First Edition

First published in Great Britain by Andersen Press Ltd.

ISBN 0-316-47328-6

Library of Congress Catalog Card Number 91-52560
Library of Congress Cataloging-in-Publication information is available.

10 9 8 7 6 5 4 3 2 1

Color separations made by Photolitho AG, Gossau, Zürich
Printed and bound in Italy by Grafiche AZ, Verona

THE GOLDEN SNOWFLAKE

by Françoise Joos
Illustrated by Frédéric Joos

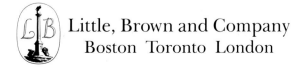

Little, Brown and Company
Boston Toronto London

Once, a long time ago, there lived a little snowman named Hector. Like all snowmen at that time, Hector lived in a vast and very cold country called the Frozen Land.

One night, before bed, Hector's mother told him the story
of the golden snowflake.

"Every hundred years," she said, "somewhere among the millions of white snowflakes that fall, there is one little, golden flake that shines like the sun. If a snowman finds a flake like this," she continued, "he is the luckiest snowman alive, because from that moment on, nothing can make him melt."

"Is it true, Mother?" Hector asked.

"If you believe hard enough," she answered, "wonderful things sometimes happen."

That night Hector stared at the falling snow. He was sure he saw something glitter and fall from the sky.

The next morning, Hector asked all his friends to come
with him and look for the golden snowflake. But they
couldn't be bothered. "Silly old Hector," cried Basil.
"You'll believe anything."
"All right then, I'll go on my own," said Hector.

Before he left, Hector's parents warned him to keep away from dangerous warm things. "Be careful, my son," said his father. "We don't want you to melt."

Chouchou the owl saw Hector set off, and he flew ahead to tell Hector's forest friends that he was coming. Moose, Fox, and the others were waiting in the forest clearing when he arrived.

"Did you see anything unusual last night?" asked Hector right away. But none of the animals had noticed the glitter in the sky. Hector told them the story of the golden snowflake. "Let's all look," cried Chouchou.

Together they all hurried to Bear's house to collect some
tools and a picnic lunch. Then they ran to the spot where
Hector thought he had seen the golden snowflake fall.

They searched and sifted through piles and piles of snow.
As they looked they talked about everything that was
happening in the forest.

They were starving by the time Bear called, "Lunch
is ready." They stopped work to eat, even though they
had seen no sign of the golden snowflake yet. Bear had
brought hot chocolate in his enormous thermos for everyone — everyone except Hector, of course. He had straw-
berry ice cream instead.

The ice cream wasn't bad, but Hector sighed deeply. "If I had the golden snowflake, I could drink hot chocolate without melting," he said.

"You could do lots of things," said Fox. "You could come
on vacation with us to the beach and have a cookout."

"I'd teach you everything about bees and honey,"
said Bear.

"I'd take you to listen to the song of the wind in the great birch forest," said Moose. Everyone had special plans for Hector.

Just then, Chouchou, who was scientifically minded, said, "I think the golden snowflake is just a dream. What would you do with it if you did find it?"

"Why," said Hector, "you press the flake to your heart until you feel all warm inside. Then you will never melt again. You're wrong, Chouchou. The golden snowflake has to be real. Dreams can come true!"

Crow interrupted the conversation. "But we haven't even found the snowflake, and it's time to go home. We'll walk with you to the edge of the forest, Hector."

Even though they hadn't found anything, they had all had great fun and planned to meet the next day to look again. As Hector, feeling a little disappointed, started for home, it began to snow.

It was then, just when he least expected it, that a tiny,
golden miracle settled quietly on him.